Orange Peel's Pocket

By **Rose Lewis**

Illustrated by **Grace Zong**

Abrams Books for Young Readers
New York

To my favorite Orange Peels—Emily, Lucy, Nell, Isabelle, Maya, and of course, Ming —R. L.

For my father —G. Z.

The illustrations in this book were made using acrylic paint on paper.

The publisher would like to thank Selena Hsu for her help checking the Chinese characters used in the artwork.

Library of Congress Cataloging-in-Publication Data

Lewis, Rose A.
Orange Peel's pocket / by Rose Lewis ; illustrated by Grace Zong.
p. cm.
Summary: A five-year-old Chinese American girl sets out to learn about the place where she was born—China.

ISBN 978-0-8109-8394-6

1. Chinese Americans—Juvenile Fiction. [1. Chinese Americans—Fiction. 2. China—Fiction.] I. Zong, Grace, ill. II. Title.

PZ7.L58787Or 2010
[E]—dc22
2009023011

Text copyright © 2010 Rose Lewis
Illustrations copyright © 2010 Grace Zong
Book design by Melissa Arnst

Published in 2010 by Abrams Books for Young Readers, an imprint of ABRAMS. All rights reserved. No portion of this book may be reproduced, stored in a retrieval system, or transmitted in any form or by any means, mechanical, electronic, photocopying, recording, or otherwise, without written permission from the publisher.

Printed and bound in China
10 9 8 7 6 5 4 3 2 1

Abrams Books for Young Readers are available at special discounts when purchased in quantity for premiums and promotions as well as fundraising or educational use. Special editions can also be created to specification. For details, contact specialmarkets@abramsbooks.com or the address below.

ABRAMS
THE ART OF BOOKS SINCE 1949
115 West 18th Street
New York, NY 10011
www.abramsbooks.com

Once there was a little girl nicknamed Orange Peel. She was born in China and now lived in America.

Orange Peel had long, jet-black hair, chocolate-colored eyes, and a huge smile. Her real name was Chan Ming, but her parents nicknamed her Orange Peel because she always tried to eat the orange peel instead of the orange when she was little.

One day her kindergarten teacher posted a big map on the blackboard. "Do you know what country this is?" she asked the class. No one knew. "Why, it's China," said the teacher.

"It's GI-NOR-MOUS!" yelled the class.

"What is China like?" asked the teacher. Again no one knew. So all eyes turned to Orange Peel. Her classmates began to ask her questions.

"How many people live in China?"
"What do they wear?"
"Does everyone eat with chopsticks?"
Then one little boy asked, "Do they play
baseball there?"

Orange Peel turned bright red and said in
a whisper, "I don't know, but I'll find out."

Orange Peel decided she would ask the grown-ups she knew who were also born in China and now lived in America. They may not know answers to all these questions, but Orange Peel was sure they knew a lot of other things about China. She would do it after school when she and her mom ran errands.

That afternoon Orange Peel and her mom set out from school. Their first stop was to Mr. Fan the tailor. Mr. Fan was at his sewing machine working on a beautiful dress.

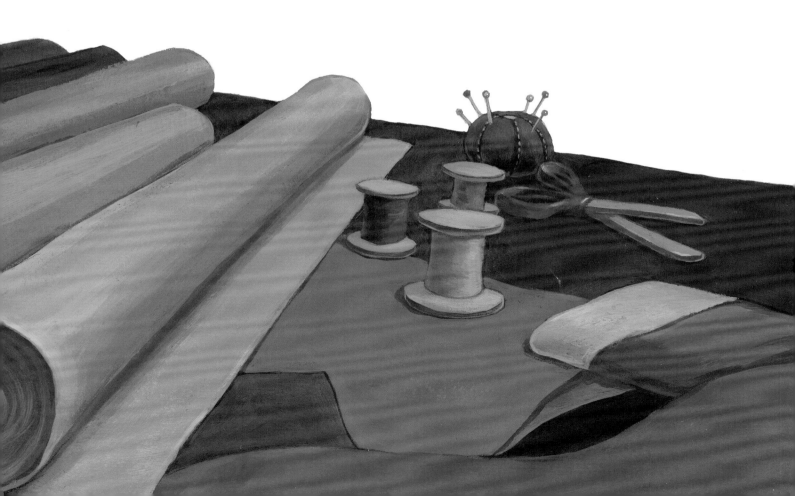

"This is made from very special silk," he said. "The best silk comes from China because the silkworms there spin a special thread found nowhere else in the world."

Orange Peel gently felt the smooth silk and smiled. She thanked Mr. Fan, and as she was saying good-bye, he secretly slipped something into Orange Peel's pocket.

Next Orange Peel and her mom stopped at Ma Sang's antiques store. Besides collecting old puppets, jade dragons, and silk calligraphy brushes, Ma Sang was a poet.

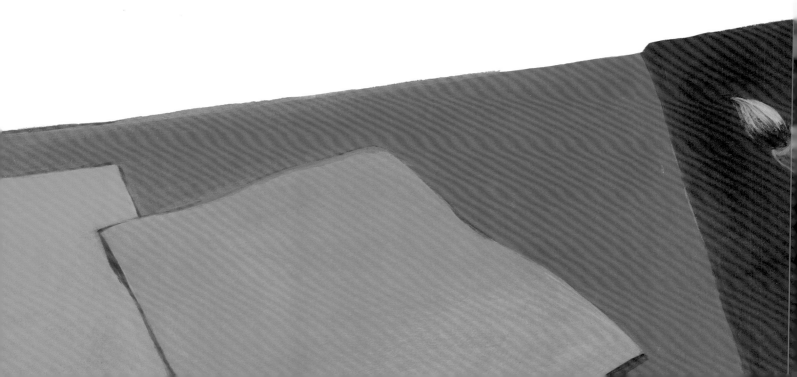

Ma Sang loved to read poems to Orange Peel, and that day he chose to read one about the beautiful mountains, lakes, and flowers in China.

Orange Peel clapped when he finished. Then she thanked Ma Sang, and as she was saying good-bye, he secretly slipped something into Orange Peel's pocket.

Listening to the beautiful descriptions of flowers made Orange Peel think of Mrs. Liu's flower shop around the corner. It was always filled with lots of flowers, but Orange Peel loved the pink peonies the best.

"See these peonies, lilies, and chrysanthemums?" said Mrs. Liu. "All of these flowers were born in China and now live in America too. People brought them here many years ago."

Orange Peel smelled the flowers one more time. Then she thanked Mrs. Liu, and as she was saying good-bye, Mrs. Liu secretly slipped something into Orange Peel's pocket.

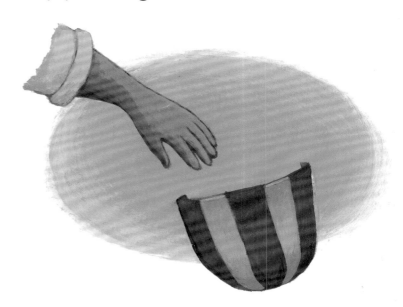

Orange Peel was hungry, so she skipped straight to Mr. Yu's noodle shop and found him stretching long noodles in the window. Mr. Yu smiled and waved Orange Peel and her mom in for what Orange Peel called Mr. Yu's "best there ever was" noodle soup. It was a secret family recipe.

"Chinese people love long noodles," Mr. Yu told Orange Peel as she slurped the noodles from her bowl. "Long noodles mean long life!"

"Yum!" exclaimed Orange Peel, and they both laughed. Orange Peel thanked Mr. Yu, and as she was saying good-bye, he secretly slipped something into Orange Peel's pocket.

Now Orange Peel was ready for dessert. She proudly told her mom she had some money in her pocket to buy the "best there ever was" ice cream at Jasmine's. When they arrived, Orange Peel excitedly told Jasmine all about her adventures and what she had learned about China. "Do you know where ice cream was invented?" Jasmine asked. Orange Peel shook her head no. "In China," Jasmine said smiling.

"And see these red knots with long tassels?" Jasmine said as she pointed to the beautiful red knots hanging along the counter. "These are signs of good luck. So every time you come here for ice cream, you will have good luck."

"Wait until the kids hear that!" Orange Peel said. She reached for the money in her pocket to pay for the ice cream.

When she pulled out her money, all of the treasures people had secretly slipped into her pocket spilled onto the floor.

"Look!" exclaimed Orange Peel.

There on the floor was a piece of silk, a poem written in Chinese, a peony, and Mr. Yu's "best there ever was" noodle soup recipe. "Now I can show AND tell the kids all about the place where I was born," Orange Peel said as she picked up her treasures and carefully put them back in her pocket.

Orange Peel thanked Jasmine, and as she was saying good-bye, Jasmine secretly slipped something into Orange Peel's pocket.

The next morning Orange Peel could feel the butterflies in her stomach on her way to school. She was very nervous.

She sat quietly with her hand pressed over her pocket. She didn't want to lose any of the things that would help her tell the story about where she was born.

Outside her classroom Orange Peel stopped and reached into her pocket to check her treasures one more time. She was surprised to discover something new among them.

It was one of the red silk knots with beautiful long tassels that had been hanging in Jasmine's ice cream shop. Orange Peel smiled because she knew it meant good luck. All at once her butterflies were gone and she wasn't nervous anymore. She smiled proudly, and holding tightly on to the red silk knot, she walked into her classroom.

Everyone was waiting to hear Orange Peel's story about the place where she was born.